Enid Blyton

THE SECRET SEVEN

WHERE ARE THE SECRET SEVEN?

Enid Blyton

THE SECRET SEVEN

WHERE ARE THE SECRET SEVEN?

Illustrated by Tony Ross

Hodder
Children's
Books

THE SECRET SEVEN

PETER JANET JACK COLIN

GEORGE PAM BARBARA

Have you read them all?

... now try the full-length **Secret Seven** mysteries:

THE SECRET SEVEN

SECRET SEVEN ADVENTURE

WELL DONE, SECRET SEVEN

SECRET SEVEN ON THE TRAIL

GO AHEAD, SECRET SEVEN

GOOD WORK, SECRET SEVEN

SECRET SEVEN WIN THROUGH

THREE CHEERS, SECRET SEVEN

SECRET SEVEN MYSTERY

PUZZLE FOR THE SECRET SEVEN

SECRET SEVEN FIREWORKS

GOOD OLD SECRET SEVEN

SHOCK FOR THE SECRET SEVEN

LOOK OUT, SECRET SEVEN

FUN FOR THE SECRET SEVEN

SCAMPER

MIX
Paper from
responsible sources
FSC® C104740

Hodder Children's Books
An imprint of Hachette Children's Group
Part of Hodder & Stoughton
Carmelite House
50 Victoria Embankment
London EC4Y 0DZ
An Hachette UK company

www.hachette.co.uk

CHAPTER ONE

'**Wuff**!' said Scamper, as he saw Peter and Janet getting out their bicycles. '**Wuff**!'

'No – you can't come with us today,' said Peter. 'Sorry,

Scamper, but we're going too fast for you. All seven of us are going to explore that old ruined house on the side of Hallows Hill. You stay here like a good dog.'

Scamper put his tail down and whined. It was too bad of the Seven to go off without him.

Peter and Janet got on their bicycles and away they

went to join the others, who were waiting for them at the top of the lane.

'Hello, Barbara, hello, Pam!' cried Janet, as she saw the other two girls who belonged to the Secret Seven.

'Hello, Colin and George!' shouted Peter. 'Where's Jack? Oh, there you are, Jack. Are we all ready – well, off we go to Hallows Hill!'

Away they went, shouting
and laughing to one another.
It was fun to be together again
on a fine Saturday morning
– no school, no work to do –
just a lovely day, a picnic and a
little exploration of a strange
old place!

CHAPTER TWO

Hallows Hill wasn't really very far if you went across the fields – but much longer by the road. The sun shone down hotly, and the Seven

began to pant as they came
to the hill on which stood
the strange old house.

'There it is!' said Colin.
'It's awfully old – and there
are strange stories about it.
Especially one about a dog.'

'About a dog? Why,
what story is there?' asked
Pam. 'Tell it to us!'

They had to get off their
bicycles to walk up the steep

path, and Colin told them the odd story.

'Well, it's said that once a dog lived there till he was very, very old – and one day his master fell down the stone stairs and couldn't move – and the dog barked all day and night for help. And now it's said that he can still be heard barking at certain times, though

the old house is ruined and empty.'

'Poor old dog,' said Janet. 'I'm sure Scamper would do the same if anything happened to us. He'd bark the place down – and his bark would go echoing down the years too! It's such a very loud one!'

Everyone laughed. Jack pointed to an old stone

tower which had just come into sight round a corner. 'Look, there's the old place,' he said. 'It's a pity it has fallen into ruins – it must have been a lovely house once.'

Jackdaws flew round the old house, and perched on the broken tower. 'We shall be able to see their nests,' said Peter. 'They build them out of twigs and I'll bet the tower

is full of old nests made of twigs and sticks!'

They were soon in the old house. It was bigger than they had imagined, and they wandered from room to room, looking all round. It was quite empty of furniture, of course – but the old stoves were still in the kitchen, and the old pump there still worked! Colin and

Jack worked the handle up and down – and water spouted into the cracked old sink!

CHAPTER THREE

'There are still some broken
dishes in the larder!' called Janet,
opening a great big door. 'My
word – what a larder! It's as big
as our sitting room at home!'

'And come and look here!' shouted Jack. 'There's an **enormous** room here – it must have been a ballroom, I should think. See, there are still mirrors all round the walls.'

They stood and looked round the silent, dusty, cobwebby room in wonder. They imagined it lit with hundreds of candles, the

floor gleaming and polished, and beautifully dressed people dancing all night through in years gone by.

Then Colin suddenly spotted something on the floor. 'Look – sweet wrappers!' he said. 'Someone besides ourselves comes here! There's a newspaper too, and greasy paper.'

'For sandwiches, I expect,'

said Peter. 'Why didn't they clear up their litter?'

'I say – come and look *here*!' called Janet, from a great old chimney place. 'If you look up this chimney you can see the blue sky ever so far up, like a little blue patch. There aren't any jackdaw nests here!'

'Why – it's big enough to stand up in!' said Pam, in wonder, standing in the

fireplace, with her head up the enormous chimney opening. 'They could have roasted a bullock here!'

They all examined the chimney place and then George gave a shout. 'There are steps at the side here – I bet they lead into an old hiding place. I'm going up to see!'

And up he went and

stumbled into a dark little room hollowed out of the great chimney stack. He felt in his pocket for his torch, and switched it on. He stared in surprise at what he saw!

'Peter! Something's hidden in here. There are lots of boxes and—'

Chapter Four

Suddenly a loud voice cut across what he was shouting. '**Hey**! What are you kids doing here? Come out of that chimney place, quick now!'

George stumbled down the steps from the little hidden room and joined the others, astonished. A tall man was standing on the hearth, looking very angry.

'I say,' began George, 'what are those boxes up in that . . .'

'Oh – so you've seen those, have you?' said the man. 'Well, that settles it! I'll have

to keep you prisoner here till I've got them away. Get into that big larder over there – all of you – quick!'

Very scared now, the Seven ran to the great larder. The enormous door was slammed on them, and they heard the key turned in the lock.

'You'll come to no harm,' called the man, 'but there

you'll stay till me and my pals
have taken our stuff away. If
kids come snooping round
they have to take what's
coming to them – it serves you
right!'

Pam began to cry, and
Janet and Barbara looked
scared.

'Cheer up!' said Peter.
'We've discovered some kind
of hiding place for stolen

goods, I expect – and that man
has shut us up to be out of the
way. I'm afraid we'll be here all
night, though – that fellow's

friends wouldn't risk removing boxes in full daylight!'

It was very boring in the great larder. A small barred window let in air, and an enormous draught blew under the door. There was a small space there, and the wind blew under it. Pam felt her feet growing colder and colder.

'I'm going to get up on this shelf out of the draught,'

she said. 'My feet are **frozen**!
Oh Peter – shall we really have
to stay here all night?'

CHAPTER FIVE

'Well, I don't see how we can get out,' said Peter. 'I only wish we could! I'd like to tell the police about this, before those boxes are removed –

but we can't tell anybody anything while we're locked up here! George – come and try and break down the door with me – and you too, Colin and Jack.'

But although they threw themselves against the door time and time again, it would not budge. The lock was old but good.

In the end they all

clambered up on the larder shelves to get out of the draught that blew under the space below the door.

Time went on. They ate all the food they had brought. They played guessing games and asked each other riddles – but oh dear, how boring it was to be shut up for hours like this!

And then Pam lifted her

head, and listened, looking rather scared. 'Listen!' she said.

'What is it?' said Colin. 'Oh that – it's only a dog barking somewhere.'

'I know – but – but don't you remember the tale you told us about the dog of long ago?' said Pam. 'Do you think it might be him? There can't be any dogs near here – it's such a lonely place!'

But before they had time to be frightened the barking came much nearer – and a brown nose snuffled suddenly under the larder door!

'It's SCAMPER!' yelled Peter, in delight. 'Scamper – you've tracked us here, even though we were on our bicycles! Oh, good dog, good dog!'

'Wuff, wuff, wuff!'

said Scamper, trying to paw
under the larder door.

CHAPTER SIX

Janet suddenly had a
wonderful idea.

'Peter! You could get hold
of Scamper's collar under the
door – there's such a big space

there. And you could tie a note on it and send him home with it to Daddy! Oh, quick, quick!'

What a marvellous idea! Peter soon carried it out. He scribbled a note on a page in his diary, tore it out, borrowed a piece of string from Jack, and tied it firmly to Scamper's collar, pulling it as far under the door as he could.

Scamper was surprised

to have his collar grabbed at, but, as usual, very willing to help the Seven! Away he went when Peter commanded him: 'Home, now! Home! Take the note to Daddy!'

'If only Daddy and the police get here in time!' said Janet. 'It will soon be dark now! Well – we must wait patiently!'

But they didn't have to

wait very long! Scamper raced home by the short cut through the fields this time, and soon delivered the note to Peter's astonished father – and in no time at all he had got out his car, collected two policemen and was speeding up the hill to the old house!

CHAPTER SEVEN

What an excitement! The
larder door was opened, and
the children poured out,
eagerly telling their story!
Colin showed where the boxes

were hidden, and the two policemen whistled when they saw them.

'They're full of priceless things stolen from the museum in the next town!' said one. 'Well – we'll wait here for the fellow who locked you in – and see who he and his friends are. You kids must go home with your father. You can't be mixed up in this – there may be some trouble!'

'*Why* can't we stay?' said Peter, indignantly. But it was no good – home they all had to go, hungry and tired, but very excited. To think they had had such an adventure on a Saturday morning!

'The men will be caught, and the goods taken back to the museum,' said Peter's father, as he drove

the children home. 'Well, I congratulate the Seven – but I'm even more pleased with Somebody Else!'

'Yes – Scamper!' cried everyone – and what a lot of pats he got. Good old Scamper! He really deserves the enormous bone he's going to get!

LOOK OUT FOR ANOTHER
SECRET SEVEN
COLOUR SHORT STORY ...

ADVENTURE ON THE WAY HOME

A big fight has broken out, and the Seven make it their mission to put a stop to it before someone gets hurt. But what's really going on between the angry people?

THE SECRET SEVEN ONLINE

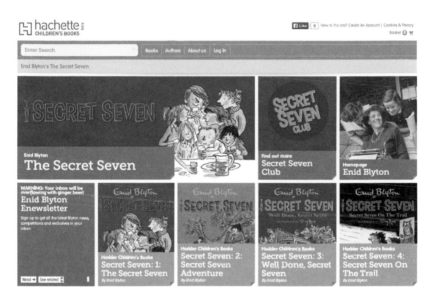

ON THE WEBSITE, YOU CAN:-

- Download and make your very own **SECRET SEVEN** door hanger
- Get tips on how to set up your own **SECRET SEVEN** club
- Find **SECRET SEVEN** snack recipes for your own club meetings
- Take the **SECRET SEVEN** quiz to see how much you really know!

Sign up to get news of brilliant competitions and more great books

AND MUCH MORE!

GO TO ... WWW.THESECRETSEVEN.CO.UK AND JOIN IN!

START YOUR
SECRET SEVEN CLUB

In each of the Tony Ross editions of The Secret Seven is a Club Token (see below). Collect any five tokens and you'll get a brilliant Secret Seven club pack — perfect for you and your friends to start your very own secret club!

GET THE SECRET SEVEN CLUB PACK:

7 club pencils   **7 club bookmarks**   **1 club poster**   **7 club badges**

Simply fill in the form below, send it in with your five tokens, and we'll send you the club pack!

Send to:

Secret Seven Club, Hachette Children's Group, Marketing Department, Carmelite House, 50 Victoria Embankment, London, EC4Y 0DZ

Closing date: 31st December 2016

TERMS AND CONDITIONS:

1) Open to UK and Republic of Ireland residents only (2) You must provide the email address of a parent or guardian for your entry to be valid (3) Photocopied tokens are not accepted (4) The form must be completed fully for your entry to be valid (5) Club packs are distributed on a first come, first served basis while stocks last (6) No part of the offer is exchangeable for cash or any other offer (7) Please allow 28 days for delivery (8) Your details will only be used for the purposes of fulfilling this offer and, if you choose [see tick box below], to send email newsletters about Enid Blyton and other great Hachette Children's books, and will never be shared with any third party.

✂ - - - - - - - -

Please complete using capital letters (UK Residents Only)

FIRST NAME:

SURNAME:

DATE OF BIRTH: DD | MM | YYYY

ADDRESS LINE 1:

ADDRESS LINE 2:

ADDRESS LINE 3:

POSTCODE:

PARENT OR GUARDIAN'S EMAIL ADDRESS:

☐ I'd like to receive a regular Enid Blyton email newsletter and information about other great Hachette Children's Group (I can unsubscribe at any time).

1 SECRET SEVEN CLUB TOKEN

www.thesecretseven.co.uk